Amelia-
Congratulations
on your first
Communion

Grandpa
May 2005

Every Child a Light

JOHN PAUL II

Every Child a Light

The Pope's Message to Young People

Edited by Jerome M. Vereb, C.P.

Wordsong
Boyds Mills Press

Special gratitute expressed to Benjamin H. Tinker and Dorothy and Loretta Vereb,
who assisted me in the research and preparation of this book,
and to *L'Osservatore Romano* for their generous permission
to reproduce the text and photographs within.
—J.V.

Copyright © 2002 by Jerome M. Vereb
All rights reserved

Published by Wordsong/Boyds Mills Press, Inc.
A Highlights Company
815 Church Street
Honesdale, Pennsylvania 18431
Printed in China
Visit our Web site at www.boydsmillspress.com

U.S. Cataloging-in-Publication Data
(Library of Congress Standards)

John Paul II, Pope, 1920–
Every child a light : the Pope's message to children by John Paul II ;
edited by Jerome M. Vereb. —1st ed.
[48] p. : col. photos. ; cm.
Summary: A collection of inspirational words for children from Pope John Paul II.
ISBN 1-56397-090-2
1. Christian children — Religious life — Juvenile literature. 2.Christian life —
Catholic authors — Juvenile literature. (1. Christian life.) I. Vereb, Jerome M. II. Title.
248.8/ 2   21   2002   AC   CIP
2001092177

First edition, 2002
The text of this book is set in 14-point Caxton Light.

10 9 8 7 6 5 4 3 2 1

Dedicated to
Donald G. Ferguson, M.D.
1923–2000
Who spent a lifetime reaching out to children.

Preface

When I participated in the Holy Year ceremonies in Rome at the end of 1999, I observed Pope John Paul II interacting frequently with children. He would reach out to them with love emanating from his face and hand gestures. He would place his hand around a child's face as he spoke. I asked Father Jerome M. Vereb, C.P., to collect words and pictures reflecting the love the Pope so clearly expressed. This book is the result.

I hope parents and teachers will use this book to help children understand God's love for them. Children will learn more about their faith and perhaps will appreciate Pope John Paul II not only as the leader of the Catholic Church but also as a warm, loving human being.

Pope John Paul II inspires people to live the way Jesus would have us live. His actions show that God loves us and is always with us. Children deserve to learn this lesson early. The words and pictures in this book mirror the way Pope John Paul II actively lives and expresses his knowledge of God's love. He shows clearly that every child is a light reflecting God's love.

Bernice E. Cullinan, Editor in Chief
Wordsong/Boyds Mills Press
June 2001

Foreword

For more than three decades, I have served the Holy See in the Pontifical Council for Social Communications. I have had a unique opportunity to observe Pope John Paul's special rapport with children. During the months of the Jubilee Year 2000, the papal commitments to celebrate the liturgy publicly or to speak to large international audiences were events that occurred almost daily. Yet they always included special time with children and young adults.

This has been equally true through all the years of the papal journeys as well as during the audiences at Rome. On every occasion, the presence of children has bespoken the value of family and a profound hope for the future for abundant blessings from God. Children are such a comfort!

Apart from my interest in journalism and photography, I bring to my daily responsibilities in the Roman Curia other identities as a mother and grandmother. I find a special comfort in discovering anew the grace of children. In this little collection, Father Jerome Vereb has gathered a few poignant moments of Pope John Paul's ministry that bring their own kind of refreshment.

Marjorie Weeke
Pontifical Council for Social Communications
Easter 2001

Introduction

During the Korean Conflict (1950–1953), a group of European and American citizens in South Korea were arrested by the invading forces of North Korea. In the course of their captivity, they were subjected to a long wintry march during which several of their number died. Captured along with them were many American military P.O.W.'s, who likewise experienced the hopelessness of captivity and the death of comrades. Among this international group of prisoners were five Carmelite nuns from France and Belgium. In their memoirs, published years later, one of the sisters wrote of the joy brought to them by the presence of young children in their midst: "Contact with children relaxes one and makes one feel younger."

In recent years, many have been impressed by the beauty and joy of exchange between Pope John Paul II and the youth of the world. Numerous biblical passages incite the Christian to hope through reference to a child. "A little child shall lead them." (Is. 11:6); "Let the little children come to Me." (Lk. 18:16); "To such as these belongs the kingdom of heaven." (Lk. 18:16).

In the season of Advent-Christmas, much emphasis is placed on the delights of childhood, but these often take the focus of fantasy. In fact, childhood carries within it all the realism of life as an adult, for every child is in the process of being formed by life to grow into a responsible adult. At the same time, no adults find fulfillment if they have lost contact with their inner child.

Spiritual childhood has been recalled for us by St. Therese of Lisieux. Many other saints have likewise recalled the characteristics of a spirituality dependent upon God as a parent figure, sustaining children with love. As St. Therese said, "It is not about how we love God or how much; what is important is that we know He loves us."

There are three qualities of childhood that must never be forgotten if the love of God is to be authentically experienced. One of these is transparency. This is a kind of honesty or genuineness that immediately identifies the presence of pretense and lies. Such honesty often amuses the adult who is subject to a child's questioning and unguarded comments.

The second characteristic is simplicity. How many of us have experienced the occasion when an elaborately planned gift was undone by a child's spontaneous fascination with the box in which the gift arrived or with the wrapping paper itself? Such simplicity is the stuff of the gospel beatitudes. Poverty of spirit brings genuine joy and peace. This kind of poverty is not destitution, but a real blessing.

Finally, there is childhood wonder. Wonder contains notes of surprise and delight. A child's sense of the unexpected brings a pleasure that he or she communicates readily. Which of us is not overwhelmed and disarmed by a baby's gurgling smile, a little girl's giggle, a young man's laugh? All of these are expressions of children's innocence and their thrill.

In an age given to sophistication yet struggling with suspicions and even a sense of cynicism, Pope John Paul's pastoral ministry has never been more effective than through his encounters with youth. The pages that follow have their own message. As one who has observed Pope John Paul's special affection toward and outreach to children and young adults, I take special pleasure in assembling these photographs and words as a mark of the depth of his self-giving.

Jerome M. Vereb, C.P.
Rome
Saints John and Paul Monastery
Easter 2001

12

Live from now on
as children of light

Dear young people,

do you know what the sacrament of Baptism does to you?

God acknowledges you as his children

and transforms your existence into a story of love with him.

He conforms you to Christ

so that you will be able to fulfill your personal vocation.

He has come to make a pact with you

and he offers you his peace.

Live from now on as children of light

who know that they are reconciled by the Cross of the Savior!

(Paris, France; August 23, 1997)

Children are the treasure
and hope of the Church

The little ones are particularly beloved of God . . .
it is to them that the kingdom of heaven
primarily belongs,
as we read in the Gospel (Mk. 10:14).
"Unless you convert and become like little children," Jesus says,
"you will not enter the kingdom of heaven." (Mt. 18:3)
At the same time,
children are the treasure
and the hope of the Church. . . .

(Tarija, Bolivia; May 13, 1988)

I bless you in the name of the Father and of the Son and of the Holy Spirit

When young people like you or older people like me

take the time to meet one another and

to show their friendship, simply and sincerely,

to help one another as best they can,

that is happiness on earth! . . .

Dear young people,

to help you live like brothers and sisters,

like friends,

with as many people as possible,

I bless you in the name of the Father

and of the Son

and of the Holy Spirit.

(Montreal, Canada; September 11, 1984)

The family prays in order to glorify and give thanks to God for the gift of life

The family celebrates the gospel of life through daily prayer,

both individual prayer and family prayer.

The family prays in order to glorify

and give thanks to God for the gift of life,

and implores his light and strength

in order to face times of difficulty and suffering without losing hope.

But the celebration that gives meaning to

every other form of prayer and worship

is found in the family's actual daily life together,

if it is a life of love and self-giving.

(Evangelium Vitae 93.1)

Even in difficult moments,
be aware that your parents
want to help you to be happy

You are the salt of the earth and the light of the world.

For each one of you, the home is a privileged place

where you love and are loved.

Your parents have called you to life

and desire to guide you in your growth.

Be grateful to them

and give thanks to the Lord!

Even in difficult moments,

be aware that your parents want to help you to be happy,

but that access to happiness also has its demands!

Like your parents, you are responsible

for life in the family and for the existence of an ever more

peaceful atmosphere,

which leaves each one enough space

to be able to give the best of himself

and to develop his personality.

(Sainte-Anne-d'Auray, France; September 20, 1996)

Look and you will see in her the face of Christ

The Pope and the Church
look upon you young people
with confidence and love.
The Church "possesses all that constitutes the strength and
the charm of youth:
the abilities to rejoice with what is beginning,
to give oneself without seeking reward,
to renew oneself,
and to embark on new conquests.
Look and you will see in her the face of Christ;
the true hero, humble and wise,
the prophet of truth and love,
the companion and friend of the young"
(Message of the Council to Youth, 6).

(Quito, Ecuador; January 30, 1985)

24

Special attention must be devoted to the children

In the family,
which is a community of persons,
special attention must be devoted to the children
by developing a profound esteem
for their personal dignity,
and a great respect and generous concern for their rights.
This is true for every child,
but it becomes all the more urgent the smaller the child is
and the more it is in need of everything
when it is sick, suffering, or handicapped.

(Familiaris Consortio n. 26)

By word and example ...
parents lead their children
to authentic freedom

It is above all in raising children

that the family fulfills its mission to proclaim the gospel of life.

By word and example,

in the daily round of relations and choices,

and through concrete actions and signs,

parents lead their children to authentic freedom,

actualized in the sincere gift of self,

and they cultivate in them respect for others,

a sense of justice,

cordial openness,

dialogue,

generous service,

solidarity,

and all the other values that help people to live life as a gift.

(Evangelium Vitae 92.4)

28

All children are important

What is beautiful about you
is that each of you looks at other children and offers a hand
with no regard for color,
social condition, or religion.
You offer your hand to one another . . .
All children are important.
All of them!

(Salvador, Brazil; October 20, 1991)

Compared with the past, youth is modernity

The Pope considers himself to be a friend
who is very close to young people and their hopes. . . .
Therefore esteeming you
and having confidence in you, he says to you:

> Compared with the past, youth is modernity;
> compared with the future,
> it is hope and the promise of discovery and innovation;
> compared with the present,
> it must be a dynamic and creative force.

(Caracas, Venezula; January 27, 1985)

You must also be open to Christ

A special characteristic of the young people of our time
is openness—
openness to the great cultural diversity of our world.
But you must also be open to Christ.
Just as he did in the case of the rich young man
in the Gospel (Mk. 10:17),
Jesus looks on you, who are rich in talents
and material things,
and he looks on you with love.
He asks you to be completely open to him
and he will never disappoint you.

(Scandinavia; June 8, 1989)

Love is patient and kind

One can say that the love for the child,

the love that springs from the very essence of fatherhood,

obliges the father to be concerned about his child's dignity.

This concern is the measure of his love,

the love of which Saint Paul was to write:

"Love is patient and kind . . .

love does not insist on its own way;

it is not irritable or resentful . . .

but rejoices in the right . . .

hopes all things,

endures all things"

and "love never ends" (1 Cor. 13:4-8).

(Dives in Misericordia 6.3)

Yes to life!

Yes to faith —
yes to life!
Recognize that a generous "yes" to Christian faith
is the purest source of fullness of life,
even for a young, forward-moving life.

(Salzburg, Austria; June 26, 1988)

You should wish to accomplish great things in your lives

The future belongs to you;

for you are the leaders of tomorrow.

As you plan and prepare for the future,

it is right that you should aspire to greatness,

that you should wish to accomplish great things in your lives.

May you never give up these desires,

but remain always men and women of high principles

and hopes.

(Saint Lucia; July 7, 1986)

I hope that you will do everything to discover your talents

How can the young person . . . today
live his or her faith?
First of all, by being aware
that there is someone who loves you
precisely because you seek to know him.
This person is Christ. . . .
One could say that youth is the time for discerning talents.
I hope that you will do everything to discover your talents.
They will lead you to respond to God's plan for each of you
and will give you the joy of cooperating
in his vast, loving design for the human race.

(Dakar, Senegal; February 21, 1992)

The Pope has a great love for children!

I talk to you with all my heart because,

following Jesus' example,

I say to you once again:

The Pope has a great love for children!

I want to see you grow up happy.

(Salvador, Brazil; October 20, 1991)

All of you have a place
and task in this Church

Right from today

you can start to make your contribution to tomorrow's Church:

a Church that does not know separation,

neither that of confessions,

nor that of generations;

a Church that offers a homeland to many

and which nevertheless makes it clear

that this world is not our permanent dwelling.

All of you have a place and task in this Church.

You build up this Church as young Christians,

as future fathers and mothers,

as believing men and women

in many professions and spheres of life.

(Vienna, Austria; September 10, 1983)

46

Young people are the source of hope for the future

The special gifts and needs of young people
deserve careful pastoral attention.
Young people are the source of hope for the future . . .
with their enthusiasm and energy,
they must be encouraged and trained to become
"leading characters in evangelization and participants
in the renewal of society."
They are evangelizers who bring the Gospel to their peers.

(Manila, Philippines; January 14, 1995)

Afterword

There is no doubt that Pope John Paul II exhibits a tender affection for children. At the opening of the Holy Door on Christmas Eve 1999, he seemed to physically touch, kiss, or pat on the head every infant that came into his path. His love extends even to absent children. I personally stood at his side as he mourned with an American mother the death of her young seminarian son by a tragic accident. These ministerial skills underscore his humanity and tenderness and, perhaps, indicate that he could have been just as at home as a pastor somewhere in rural Poland.

Yet he is the Pope! He has a philosophy that he brings to his theological instruction. Children are persons with dignity and rights. They have a mission and a responsibility. The future rests upon their shoulders. Children form their own global community now. They are drawn to each other across countries, cultures, and languages. In their innocence they are a mighty force for good.

There are indeed all kinds of children; there are children from large family circles and those born into single-child homes. Some children emerge from war-torn countries, and there are those who have been blessed with peace in their lifetime. While there are babes in their mothers' arms, there are also those who are old in age yet like a child in their inmost being.

As he has spoken in Rome and across the globe, Pope John Paul has instructed that children of every color, creed, and teaching be brought to that love that Jesus alone gives. The Pontiff's prayer for youth may be thus summarized: Incline the heart of every child on this earth with the knowledge and the freedom to be the "children of God!" May God pour forth the Holy Spirit that his glory may shine forth and all may heed the word given to the disciples: "Allow the little children to come to me and do not hinder them, for to such as these belongs the Kingdom of God. I tell you solemnly, anyone who does not welcome the Kingdom of God like a little child will never enter it" (Lk. 18:16-17).

In these words of Scripture, a sacred disclosure is found. Jesus himself is *the* Child of God. He possesses therefore a unique kinship with all other children. In turn, children everywhere are the special apostles of the Kingdom of Heaven!

Jerome M. Vereb, C.P.

48